The Boy and the North Wind

A TALE FROM NORWAY

Retold by Suzanne I. Barchers • Illustrated by Laura Jacobsen

RED CHAIR PRESS

Please visit our website at **www.redchairpress.com**.
Find a free catalog of all our high-quality products for young readers.

 For a free activity page for this story, go to
www.redchairpress.com and look for Free Activities.

The Boy and the North Wind

Publisher's Cataloging-In-Publication Data
(Prepared by The Donohue Group, Inc.)

Barchers, Suzanne I.
The boy and the north wind : a tale from Norway / retold by Suzanne I. Barchers ;
illustrated by Laura Jacobsen.
p. : col. ill. ; cm. -- (Tales of honor)
Summary: When a cold north wind blows away the flour carried by the baker's
young son, the boy sets out on a journey to insist that it be returned. This tale
demonstrates the value of never giving up and appreciating the gifts of nature.
Includes special educational sections: Words to know, What do you think?, and
About Norway.
Interest age level: 006-010.
ISBN: 978-1-937529-72-7 (lib. binding/hardcover)
ISBN: 978-1-937529-56-7 (pbk.)
ISBN: 978-1-936163-88-5 (eBook)
1. Perseverance (Ethics)--Juvenile fiction. 2. Boys--Juvenile fiction. 3. Winds--Juvenile fiction.
4. Folklore--Norway. 5. Perseverance (Ethics)--Fiction. 6. Boys--Fiction. 7. Winds--Fiction.
8. Folklore--Norway. I. Jacobsen, Laura. II. Title.

PZ8.1.B37 Bo 2013

398.2/73/09481   2012951558

This series first published by:
Red Chair Press LLC   PO Box 333   South Egremont, MA 01258-0333

Printed in the United States of America

1 2 3 4 5 18 17 16 15 14

$\mathcal{A}$ mother wanted to make a loaf of bread.

"Son," she said, "take this bowl and go to the miller and buy some flour. Here's a coin for the flour. Hurry back!"

"Alright, Mother," said the boy. "I'll be back soon."

The boy walked to the mill and bought the flour. He carried the bowl carefully, not wanting to lose a speck of flour. Just as he neared the cottage, the North Wind whisked by, blowing the flour to the four corners of the world. The boy ran the rest of the way home.

"Mother! Mother!" the boy cried. "I went to the miller and bought the flour. But just as I came near the house, the North Wind blew the flour away. What shall we do?"

"Son, here is another coin. Go back to the miller and buy more flour. Try to be more careful this time," said the mother.

The boy hurried to the miller's shop and
bought more flour. He walked with great care,
watching for any signs of the North Wind. Just
before arriving safely home, the North Wind
blustered by again. The entire bowl of flour
was scattered out of sight.

"Mother! Mother!" the boy cried. "It happened again! I was almost home and the North Wind blew the flour away. I am so sorry, Mother."

Mother sighed, "Son, this is my last coin.
Return again to the miller's shop. But if you
lose the flour again, we will go hungry."

Once again the boy took the bowl to the mill
and traded the last coin for a bowl of flour.
And once again the North Wind blew the flour
to the four corners of the world. This time,
however, the boy did not return home.

"Enough!" the boy said. "I am going to go to
the North Wind and demand that he give me
back my three bowls of flour!"

The boy dropped the empty bowl. Then he sat and thought for a while. He decided that the most likely place for the North Wind to live would be high on the mountain to the north. He set out, walking without stopping.

Upon reaching the mountaintop, he greeted the North Wind.

"Good day," said the boy.

"What brings you here, young man?" the North Wind asked.

"My mother sent me to the miller's shop to buy flour for bread. I was almost home, when you came along and blew the flour away. I ask only that you return the three bowls of flour."

"I am afraid I cannot do that, Son," the North Wind responded. "You see, all that flour has been scattered to the four corners of the world. However, I will give you something so that you will never be hungry again. This is my magic tablecloth. Whenever you say to it, 'Cloth, spread yourself,' it will be covered with the finest of food."

"Thank you!" said the boy. "My mother will be so happy to have this."

The boy, having spent the day walking to
the top of the mountain, was very tired. He
stopped at an inn, begging for a place to sleep
for the night. The innkeeper, taking pity on the
young boy, told him he could sleep in a back
room. Having had no food all day, the boy
decided it was time to try out the tablecloth.

"Cloth, spread yourself!" the boy cried. In the twinkling of an eye, the cloth was covered with a feast. He hardly knew where to start. As the boy ate, the innkeeper spied through the keyhole.

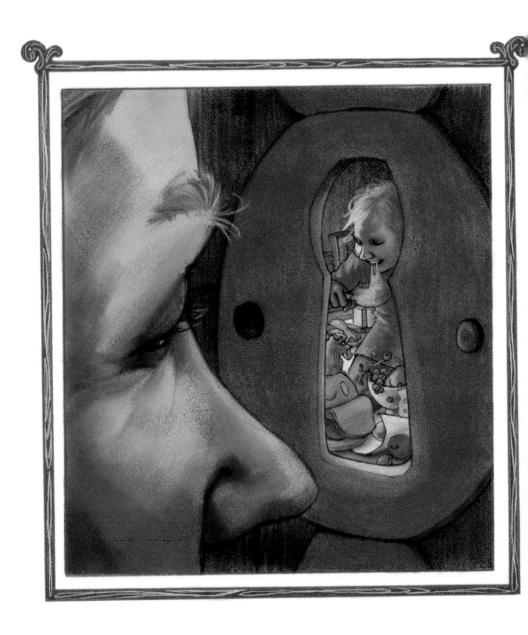

"That tablecloth must be magic," he whispered. "I must have it for myself. Think of the money I can make!"

That night, the boy used the cloth as a blanket and dreamed of endless feasts. He was so sound asleep that he didn't notice the innkeeper replacing the cloth with a quilt.

The next morning the boy was distraught at the loss of the tablecloth. Not wanting to go home empty handed, he went back up the mountain and found the North Wind.

"The cloth is truly magical, North Wind. But it was stolen. I am not sure, but I think the thief might be the innkeeper," the boy said.

"Take this magic staff," North Wind replied.
"All you must do is go back to the inn and say,
'Staff, dance!' The staff will dance on the toes
of the thief. It will stop once you have the cloth
back."

The boy thanked the North Wind and returned
to the inn. He found the innkeeper and his
guests eating a grand feast made by the magic
tablecloth. He wasted no time. "Staff, dance!"

The staff danced right over to the innkeeper. It danced on his toes! No matter what the innkeeper did, the staff bounced up and down on his toes!

"Please! Stop this staff!" the innkeeper cried.

"Return to me what is mine and the staff will stop," said the boy.

"Yes! Take the cloth! Just make it stop," begged the thief.

23

The boy pulled the cloth out from under the dishes. As he bundled it up, the staff danced away from the innkeeper. It danced out the door and right back to the North Wind!

The boy walked home without further delay.
As he entered the house, his mother hugged
him and said, "Where have you been? I found
the empty bowl and have been so worried."

"Mother, I lost the flour. But I got something better from the North Wind," the boy said excitedly. "Just watch. 'Cloth, spread yourself!'"

Just like before, a wonderful feast appeared.
The boy and his mother never went hungry
again. And they never forgot to give thanks
for the gifts from the North Wind.

blustered: when wind blows very hard and with a lot of noise

distraught: deeply upset and troubled

miller: a person who works in a grain mill, often making bread

scattered: thrown in random and different directions

WHAT DO YOU THINK?

Question 1: The wind blew the flour out of the boy's bowl each time he tried to carry it home. What did his mother say would happen if he lost the flour a third time?

Question 2: What did the North Wind give the boy to take back to his mother? Why did he not return with the lost flour?

Question 3: Do you think the boy and his mother were happy with the gift from the North Wind? Why?

Question 4: The winds in Norway can be very cold and strong. Think about a feature of nature where you live. How would you describe it in a story?

About Norway

The ancient kingdom of Norway extends from the North Sea to more than 300 miles (483 km) above the Arctic Circle. From the coast, the land rises sharply to majestic mountains, wind-swept plateaus, and large glacier fields. The people of Norway have a strong connection to their land and the seasons. In winter, the country is often snow-covered with strong north winds.

About the Author

After fifteen years as a teacher, Suzanne Barchers began a career in writing and publishing. She has written over 100 children's books, two college textbooks, and more than 20 reader's theater and teacher resource books. She previously held editorial roles at Weekly Reader and LeapFrog and is on the PBS Kids Media Advisory Board. Suzanne also plays the flute professionally – and for fun – from her home in Stanford, CA.

About the Illustrator

Laura Jacobsen has been drawing, painting, and doodling her whole life. Her work has appeared in many kids' magazines and books. Laura's two dogs, Hopper and Lucy, keep her company in her Gilbert, Arizona, studio.